Shopkins™

Once you shop...You can't stop!

A MERRY SHOPKINS CHRISTMAS

©2013 Moose. Shopkins™ logos, names and characters are licensed trademarks of Moose Enterprise Pty Ltd.

All rights reserved. Scholastic Children's Books, Euston House, 24 Eversholt Street, London NW1 1DB, UK

A division of Scholastic Ltd
London ~ New York ~ Toronto ~ Sydney ~ Auckland ~ Mexico City ~ New Delhi ~ Hong Kong

First published in the US by Scholastic Inc, 2016
Published in the UK by Scholastic Ltd, 2016

ISBN 978 14071 7063 3

Printed in Italy

2 4 6 8 10 9 7 5 3 1

All rights reserved

Papers used by Scholastic Children's Books are made from woods grown in sustainable forests.

www.scholastic.co.uk

It's Christmas Eve in Shopville. The sale signs are twinkling. Snow is falling like powdered sugar. And the Shopkins are getting ready for the Christmas Eve Festival.

Cheeky Chocolate, Apple Blossom, Strawberry Kiss and Lippy Lips practise their Christmas carol.

♪ "DECK THE AISLES FOR SHOPKINS CHRISTMAS,
FA-LA-LA-LA-LA, LA-LA-LA-LA.
SOON THE STORE WILL LOOK DELICIOUS!
FA-LA-LA-LA-LA, LA-LA-LA-LA!"

"Ooh, ooh, is it time for my solo?" asks Lippy Lips.
Lippy has been practising a big solo for weeks. But she's kept it completely under wrappers as a surprise for her friends.

"Not yet," says Apple. "First we have to make Small Mart look berry and bright!"

Apple tells all the Shopkins what they need to do to get Small Mart ready for tonight.

Spilt Milk sets all of Small Mart's freezers to the lowest
level – Arctic Blast. That will make it snow all over the store.
"Easy cheesy frozen-peasy," says Spilt Milk. "Getting things chilly
is right up my aisle!"

Spilt Milk does *too* good of a job making snow. In fact, she's made a blizzard!

"Whoa!" she cries. "This snow is more slippery than a frozen banana peel!"

Meanwhile, Strawberry Kiss wraps presents. She chooses just the right paper and bows for each one.

"These presents are sure to fill everyone with holiday cheer!" she says.

Cheeky Chocolate tries to steal a glimpse of what's inside the gift boxes.

"No, no, you sneaky Cheeky!" says Strawberry. "Don't spoil the surprise!"

"Did someone say, *surprise*?" asks Lippy. "That must mean it's time for my solo!"

Lippy picks up the microphone and gets ready to sing.

"Wait – not just yet!" cries Apple. "First we have to decorate the tree."

"*Ohhh,*" says Lippy. She's not sure she can wait until tonight.

Apple hangs shiny decorations on every branch until the tree looks just right.

"Kooky, can you put the star at the top?" Apple asks.

"Um, okay," says Kooky.

Kooky climbs a tower of gift boxes to reach the top of the tree.

The boxes sway left . . . they sway right . . . Kooky topples towards the tree!

The star lands at the top just before Kooky tumbles safely to the ground. It's a Shopkins Christmas Miracle!

"That was close," says Apple. "Good job, Kooky!"
"Thanks." Kooky laughs. "I'm just glad I didn't crumble in the tumble!"

Soon it is night-time. All the Shopkins gather at the centre of Small Mart for the Christmas Eve Festival.

"Now is it time for my solo?" asks Lippy.

"Just a little while longer," says Apple. "First it's time to open presents!"

"*Ohhh*," groans Lippy. She doesn't want to wait any longer! Meanwhile, Strawberry Kiss is as pleased as punch with how pretty the gifts look. "Didn't I do the sweetest wrapping job you've ever seen?" she gushes.

Suddenly, one of the presents moves . . .
"Uh, Strawberry?" asks Apple. "What
exactly did you wrap in the gift boxes?"

Surprise! Out pops Dum Mee Mee! She sneaked into one of the presents while Cheeky was distracting Strawberry Kiss. "Wow!" exclaims Strawberry. "Dum Mee Mee, you surprised me!"

"Surprise? SURPRISE?" cries Lippy. "NOW is it time for my solo?"
Apple smiles. "Yes, Lippy. It's finally time."
"Oh, thank groceries!" exclaims Lippy.
The Shopkins begin their Christmas carol together.

Lippy sings her solo with all her might.
"FA-LA-LA-LA-LA, LA LA . . . LA . . . LAAAAAAAAAAAA!"

Pop! Pop! Pop!
Lippy's solo is so loud, it breaks all the lights in Small Mart!
"Wow," Apple says. "That was certainly . . . the biggest surprise of the night!"
Lippy beams. "Wasn't it? Merry Christmas, everyone!"

It is the season for good cheer and sweet surprises. Even if it's a bit off-key.
Merry Christmas from the Shopkins!